BATMAN™
STRIKES BACK

Adapted by R. J. Cregg
Illustrated by Patrick Spaziante
Based on the screenplay written by Heath Corson
Batman created by Bob Kane with Bill Finger

Simon Spotlight
New York London Toronto Sydney New Delhi

SIMON SPOTLIGHT
An imprint of Simon & Schuster Children's Publishing Division
1230 Avenue of the Americas, New York, New York 10020
This Simon Spotlight paperback edition August 2016
All rights reserved, including the right of reproduction in whole or in part in any form.
SIMON SPOTLIGHT and colophon are registered trademarks of Simon & Schuster, Inc.
For information about special discounts for bulk purchases, please contact Simon & Schuster Special Sales at 1-866-506-1949 or business@simonandschuster.com.
Manufactured in the United States of America 0716 LAK
10 9 8 7 6 5 4 3 2 1
ISBN 978-1-4814-7835-9
ISBN 978-1-4814-7836-6 (eBook)

It's a dark night in Gotham City, and high society is flocking to the opening of the Aviary, the city's newest and tallest building. Normally Bruce Wayne would be patrolling the streets as Batman, his super hero secret identity, but this is a special occasion.

"I'll bet you'll get a nice view of the Midas Heart comet when it passes by tomorrow night," Bruce says to the Aviary's owner, Oswald Cobblepot.

"Indeed," Cobblepot says, with a sneer.

Cobblepot takes the stage. "Ladies and gentlemen," he screeches. "Welcome to my little perch at the top of the Aviary. I'm proud to present our company's latest invention—unmanned robotics!" he announces as a robotic tiger, wolf, and bat rise behind him.

Over the applause he can hear a few people laughing at him. "Weird little penguin," someone says.

"That's it!" he shouts. Oswald Cobblepot is not one to be teased. He hits a button on his umbrella and the Cyber Animals come to life, growling and pushing the guests toward the elevator. As Bruce Wayne makes his exit, he's sure he's seen those robots before.

The next day Batman calls a meeting with his fellow super heroes: Green Arrow, Nightwing, Red Robin, and The Flash. Batman knows Cobblepot is up to something. On the Batcomputer, Batman pieces together clues. He discovers the Penguin has been setting up a force field around the Aviary.

"This antenna is built to aim at something," says Green Arrow, pointing to the top of the Aviary.

Batman makes the connection. "The Midas Heart," he says, "Cobblepot is going to crash the comet into Gotham City."

Suddenly, the Penguin's transmitters turn on, activating the force field. A familiar face appears on all the screens in Gotham City.

"Greetings," says the villain. "I am Oswald Cobblepot . . . but you may call me the Penguin!" A crowd gathers to watch the screens. "The Midas Heart is no longer going to whiz past Earth. I have altered its path with my tractor beam. And now I will crash it into Gotham City," he says.

The crowd gasps.

"Don't worry about me," continues the Penguin. "I'll be safely behind my force field, and after you are gone, I will live happily, wealthily . . . and free of you. Good-bye, Gotham City . . . forever."

▲77.20
▼85.20

Batman changes into his knightstalker suit. He is the protector of Gotham City, and tonight he and his friends are going to put the Penguin's plan on ice!

In the center of the city, the Gotham City Police Department opens fire on the force field.

"You're going to have to do better than that," the Penguin squawks from inside the Aviary. "This force field was built to withstand a collision with a comet!"

Within seconds Batman arrives in his Batwing.

"Take your best shot, Batman," says the Penguin.

Batman activates his knightstalker suit. It crackles with electricity and surrounds Batman with an amber energy field.

"That's impossible!" screams the Penguin as Batman walks straight through the force field.

Inside the force field Batman takes off his knighstalker suit.
The Penguin's Cyber Animal Army fills the street.

"Ace, come!" Batman calls. He has hidden one of his own Cyber Wolves in the Penguin's pack. Ace leaps foward and transforms into a motorcycle. Batman has taken this Cyber Animal and reprogrammed it to do new tricks.

"*Fowl* play!" cries the Penguin. "Destroy him, my Cyber Children!"

"Flash, get that force field down," Batman says through his communicator as he races off to escape.

With Batman on the run, The Flash zips onto the scene. "You got this," he tells himself. He is wearing a special device that works with his superspeed. The device fires up as he runs faster and faster. Just as he is about to crash into the force field, the device lets him slip through. "I'm in!" he yells.

"Well done," says Batman over his communicator. "Now, all you need to do is take out a receiver."

The Flash dashes into action. The Cyber Tigers nip at his heels. The Flash is fast, but so are they. They whip at him with their metal tails.

"Great, they upgraded!" The Flash complains just as he finds a receiver.

"Here, boy!" The Flash calls, tossing a receiver into the metal fangs of a Cyber Tiger. *Crunch!* The force field goes down.

Now Batman's other super hero buddies can join the fight! Nightwing swipes at Cyber Wolves with his electric batons. From the rooftops Green Arrow fires perfect shots. "Don't worry, Bats," he says to Batman. "We've got your back." They take out the Penguin's Cyber Wolves left and right.

"Well, that's my cue to exit," says the Penguin as he moves toward his escape pod. "I bid you *adieu*," he says to his henchmen just before blasting off into the sky.

"Penguin's getting away!" cries Green Arrow as he fires at the escape pod.

"Where's my computer virus?" Batman asks through his communicator. He struggles as a Cyber Wolf clamps down on his wrist.

"Almost there," says Red Robin from the Batcave. Moments later, the upload is complete and the Cyber Animal Army suddenly collapses.

"The virus worked!" says Batman. "Good job, Robin."

"Now what about the giant flaming rock?" asks Green Arrow. The heroes turn their attention toward the Midas Heart comet, still plummeting toward Gotham City. "Can we reverse the tractor beam?" asks Nightwing.

"I have a better idea," says Batman. "Here's what I need . . ."

Nightwing collects parts for a stronger tractor beam. The Flash moves the force-field receivers to surround the entire city. Green Arrow finds a power source for the controls.

They create a bigger force field that covers all of Gotham City and activate their tractor beam. "So this new tractor beam is going to shoot that comet back into space?" asks Green Arrow.

"No," says Batman. "It's going to pull it at us faster."

"Right . . . wait, *what*?!" yells Green Arrow.

"If my calculations are correct, we should be safe," says Batman.

"Brace for impact. Here it comes!" shouts Green Arrow.

"Oh man, I can't look!" says The Flash as the comet strikes the force field.

Kaboom! The comet explodes into tiny pieces. Chunks of burning rock bounce off of the force field and fall harmlessly into the water.

The people of Gotham City cheer.

The heroes stand proudly and look out over the city they saved. With all their skills, they make a great team.

"It's a shame that Penguin got away," says Green Arrow.

But far away an escape pod crash-lands in the darkness. The Penguin gets out, grumbling to himself. He was supposed to land someplace warm, not here. "Nothing ever works like it's supposed to," he complains.

Thanks to Batman and his friends, the Penguin ended up on ice after all!